FROG, WHERE ARE YOU?

Sequel to A BOY, A DOG AND A FROG

by Mercer Mayer

DIAL BOOKS FOR YOUNG READERS
New York

For Phyllis Fogelman,
a dear friend, who inspired
the creation of the faded
pink dummy.

Published by Dial Books for Young Readers
A division of E. P. Dutton | A division of New American Library
2 Park Avenue, New York, New York 10016
Copyright © 1969 by Mercer Mayer. All rights reserved.
Library of Congress Catalog Card Number: 72-85544
Printed in Hong Kong by South China Printing Co.
COBE
8 10 12 14 15 13 11 9